The Mystery of the Phantom Pony

By Lynn Hall
Illustrated by Marie DeJohn

Previously titled *The Mystery of Plum Park Pony*

A STEPPING STONE BOOK

Random House 🏠 New York

Text copyright © 1980, 1993 by Lynn Hall
Illustrations copyright © 1993 by Marie DeJohn
Cover art copyright © 1993 by Ruth Sanderson
Published in the United States by Random House, Inc., New York, and simultaneously
in Canada by Random House of Canada Limited, Toronto. Originally published in
different form in 1980 by Garrard Publishing Company as *The Mystery of Plum
Park Pony.*

Library of Congress Cataloging-in-Publication Data
Hall, Lynn.
[Mystery of Plum Park pony]
The mystery of the phantom pony / by Lynn Hall ; illustrated by Marie DeJohn.
p. cm. — (A Stepping Stone book)
"Previously titled: The mystery of Plum Park pony."
SUMMARY: Searching the amusement park for a pony only Susan has seen, Susan and
Kent track it to the Tunnel of Terror. As they realize the pony is trapped inside, the
train begins its test run.
ISBN 0-679-84335-3 (pbk.) — ISBN 0-679-94335-8 (lib. bdg.)
[1. Horses—Fiction.   2. Amusements parks—Fiction.   3. Mystery and detective
stories.]   I. DeJohn, Marie, ill.   II. Title.   III. Series.
PZ7.H1458Myo   1993   [Fic]—dc20   93-7149

Manufactured in the United States of America   10 9 8 7 6 5 4 3

Contents

1

A Mystery Pony

It was a Saturday morning in May and the sun was shining. Susan came out of her house smiling. She had a lot to smile about. Susan had a job to do this morning, and it was the best job in the world.

She jumped the hedge into Kent's yard. He was her best friend and not just because he lived next door. Kent was fun to be with. He had good ideas, and when Susan had better ideas he was a good sport about it. And when Susan got too bossy he didn't get mad. He just ignored her. So they got along fine.

Kent was just coming out the door, hopping on one foot to tie his shoelaces. "Hurry up," Susan called, heading for the street. He had to run to keep up with her, his laces flopping.

Their street was the last one at the edge of town. Kent and Susan thought their two houses were in the best spot on the street because they were right across from the entrance to Funland. On summer evenings the lights from the Tilt-O-Whirl flashed across their yards. They could hear the merry-go-round's music and screams and clatter from the roller coaster.

But for Susan the very best part of Funland was the ponies. They walked in patient circles in the pony ride at the corral, looking at her with big eyes under shaggy manes, and she loved them. She loved their dusty fragrance, their moist breath against her cheek. She loved to bury her hand in the warm places under their manes, and to hug their necks.

But most of all she loved to ride them. And

today...Today her excitement was almost too strong to hold in. Today she had a job to do, and that job was riding the ponies!

The big entrance gate to Funland had been closed since last fall. But there was a lot going on behind it this morning. Men were at work painting, raking, and getting ready for the new season. There had been a storm last night, and they were picking up small branches blown down from the trees at the edge of the park. Rain puddles glistened here and there on the ground.

Susan called through the gate to one of the men. "Would you please let us in?"

"We're not open yet," the man called back. "No kids allowed."

"But we have a job. We're helping Jackson with the ponies. He told us to come."

The man came closer. He looked as though he couldn't make up his mind whether to believe Susan or not.

Susan said, "Jackson told us that we should

come right before opening day. He needs help with the ponies. They get frisky during the winter with nobody to ride them. Jackson's too big. He wants us to ride them so they'll be tame enough for the little kids."

"Well, okay," the man said, unlocking the gate. "But don't touch anything."

"What does he think we're going to touch?" Kent muttered to Susan. He knelt and quickly tried to double-knot his laces. They were long and floppy and seemed to have a life of their own.

But Susan was too busy looking around to answer. She loved Funland at any time. But today, with no one in the park but the workmen, it had a new kind of excitement. It was as if it were here just for her and Kent to enjoy. The grass had a special sparkle to it. The plum trees were pink with blossoms. And there, near the grove of oak trees at the back of the park, were the ponies. Susan started to run toward them, but she slowed down when she got close.

She didn't want to scare them.

The ponies were tied to trees on long ropes, so they could move around and find grass to eat. Each of the six ponies had mowed a circle around its tree. Behind them was an old tin shed, where Jackson sat on a broken chair, dozing in the sun.

During the winter, Susan and Kent had talked about Jackson a lot. They had tried to figure out whether "Jackson" was his first name or last. They had tried to guess whether he was really old, like a grandfather, or whether he just looked old because he was so messy. There was one thing about Jackson they agreed on. He was the laziest person they knew.

Jackson opened his eyes when they ran up to him. These were the only muscles he moved.

"We came to ride the ponies," Susan said. "Remember last fall? You told us if we came the day before the park opened, we could ride—"

Jackson waved toward the ponies. "Well,

hop to it," he said. "These ponies need a lot of riding. They're wild when spring comes."

The six fat ponies grazed quietly. They were anything but wild, and Susan knew it. But she wasn't going to argue.

"Where are their saddles?" she asked. "In the shed?"

Jackson nodded. "But don't use the saddles," he said. "Ride them bareback. That's the way to learn to be a good rider."

Susan and Kent looked at each other. "He's just too lazy to saddle the ponies for us," Susan whispered to Kent. But bareback was more fun anyway. They grabbed two bridles and studied them. "This metal part goes in the mouth," Susan said, touching the bit. "And I think this part goes behind their ears, and this little strap buckles under their chin," she finished triumphantly, her eyes challenging Kent to disagree. Since he knew less about bridles than Susan, he just shrugged.

It wasn't so easy getting the bridles on

the ponies, Susan found. The first pony kept spitting out the bit before she could work the top part over his ears. But after a while she got better at it, and the second pony was easier.

Even though the ponies were small, they were so fat that Susan had to kick and grunt and jump hard to get herself up onto hers. He was a dusty black with a mane that fell in all directions. Kent was already aboard his pinto and trotting away.

"Let's go, boy," she said, turning his head and tapping with her heels. The pony didn't much want to leave his grass, but started off at a slow jog. At first it was jouncy and a little scary, but Susan grabbed a fistful of mane, sat up straight, and relaxed. Soon the bouncing smoothed and she was completely comfortable.

Riding was the best, Susan thought. The ponies trotted happily up and down the gravel roads and paths of the park. They seemed to be enjoying themselves as much as Susan and Kent.

When their ponies began to get tired and sweaty, Susan and Kent took them back, tied them to their trees, and rode two more. Then they rode the last two. Kent went to tell Jackson they were finished. As Susan was tying up her last pony and wishing there were more to ride, something caught her eye.

It was a pony—one that Susan had never seen before. She was grazing some distance from the others, and she wasn't wearing a halter, as they were. She looked up as Susan came close.

"Wow!" Susan whispered.

This was the prettiest pony she had ever seen. She was a bright red bay, with a gleaming black mane and tail. Her head was elegant and her legs were dainty.

Quickly, before Kent came back from talking with Jackson, Susan moved toward her, still carrying the bridle.

The huge dark eyes watched Susan, alert but fearless. When Susan held out her hand, the pony stretched out her muzzle to sniff. Susan stood very still.

The velvety muzzle brushed her arm, nudged her shoulder, sniffed at her hair. The warm breath tickled Susan's ear and made her want to giggle. She reached up and stroked the warm, satin neck. Then she slipped the bridle on and buckled it into place.

But Susan didn't jump onto her back. Something made her pause, some quality about the pony that was like royalty. When she pictured her in the ride concession, tied to the wheel that led the other ponies around and around in their endless circle, it made Susan shake her head. Wrong! This pony shouldn't be carrying crying toddlers and thoughtless rein-jerkers in plodding circles all summer. This pony should...fly!

Before she had time to think about what she was doing, Susan was on the pony's back.

It felt perfect.

After the other ponies, riding this one was like floating on a cloud. The bay moved with steps so smooth that Susan's hair didn't even bounce. Girl and pony cantered among the trees like a pair of dancers. If Susan leaned to the left or right, the pony leaned with her, turning with absolute smoothness.

Looking down, Susan could see that the pony carried her head proudly. Her ears were alert, her neck arched. The dainty little hooves came up high with every step.

Susan thought, "She's almost like...a show horse! Or like those fancy ponies we saw at the state fair last summer. They pulled little carts and pranced around the ring just like she's doing now. I wonder..."

Susan slowed the pony to a walk and started back toward Jackson's shed. She was eager to ask Jackson what this beautiful show pony was doing among his fat little Shetlands. But she was not at all eager to get down from the beautiful pony's back. It had been a magic ride.

But even magic rides have to end. Susan slid off the pony, unbuckled her bridle, and slipped it off the lovely head. Then she remembered that the pony had been wearing no halter. She wrapped the reins around the red neck and began searching through the grass for the missing halter.

It wasn't there. "Jackson," she called, "I can't find this pony's halter."

From the shed came only loud snores.

Susan called Kent. "Will you give me a hand

here? I can't find—"

Just then the roller coaster, on a trial run, roared along its track overhead. The pony jerked back suddenly, pulled free, and ran. "Stop!" shouted Susan.

But it was no use. Like a flash of red lightning, the pony bolted around a cotton-candy wagon and disappeared. Susan ran after her, but when she got around the corner of the wagon, the pony was nowhere in sight. She walked back to the tin shed, where she found Kent and Jackson.

"What's all the yelling about?" Jackson asked.

"One of the ponies got away!" Susan said.

Jackson looked around. There were six ponies tied to six trees. "They're all here," he said.

"No," Susan wailed. "The pretty one got away! The beautiful bay."

Jackson looked at her. "I don't have a bay," he said.

2

The Pony Disappears

"But she was right here," Susan told them. "Kent, you saw her, didn't you?"

"I didn't see her," Kent said. "I heard you yelling, and I came as fast as I could. But I didn't see a bay pony. What is a bay pony, anyway?"

"A red one, and I didn't make her up," Susan said. "She was here. I rode her. And I'm going to go find her. Are you coming?" she asked Kent.

"Sure," said Kent. Susan smiled. She knew that whether Kent believed in the pony or not, he'd look for her. He loved a challenge.

Jackson went back to his chair and sat down heavily. He looked as though just the thought of chasing a pony made him tired.

"This way," Susan said. Kent followed as she ran toward the dim shade of the oak grove. Dotted with picnic tables and stone barbecue grills, the grove was the quietest part of the park—and Susan's favorite place, except for the pony corral.

There was only one building back here—the long shed-like building that held the Tunnel of Terror. The building's front faced the midway and was brightly painted with spooks and monsters. Its back marked the outer edge of Funland.

As they came closer to the building, Susan and Kent slowed to a walk, then stopped. They could see the whole picnic grove from here. They knew there was no place in it that could hide a bay pony. She wasn't there.

"She must have gone out on the midway,"

Kent said. "Let's look there." They started out
in that direction.

The midway was bright in the May sun-
shine. Painters and mechanics were working on many of the rides. The Tilt-O-Whirl
was running, its empty cars spinning through
the air.

Susan and Kent ran from one ride to

another, asking the workmen if they'd seen the pony. No one had.

They made the full circle of the midway and came back to the Tunnel of Terror. In front of the building, the little four-car train that carried passengers through the tunnel was standing in the sunlight. It ran on a narrow track that looped out of the building onto the passenger platform, then back inside. At the edge of the platform was a big red lever that started and stopped the train.

"Maybe the tunnel-ride man saw her go by," Susan said.

They went around to the side of the building. Here a door stood open, showing a tiny room full of gears and levers that ran the train. Two men were inside. One was the tunnel-ride operator. Susan remembered him from last year. The other man wore mechanic's overalls. He was working on some of the equipment.

The ride operator looked up at Susan and Kent and grinned. "Who let you two in?" he asked in a joking voice. "I bet you're looking for free rides, aren't you?"

"No, we're looking for a pony," Susan told him. "Did you see a red pony go by here a little while ago?"

"No, but I saw a pink elephant," the man said, laughing. Susan turned away. "Get serious!" she thought. She had to find that pony.

"How about a free ride on the train?" he offered. Kent hesitated. The Tunnel of Terror was his favorite ride.

The man said, "We're going to start her up soon—first time this season. We'll run her around the track to be sure everything's okay. You can come if you want."

"We have to find her, Kent," said Susan. Kent sighed.

"We have to find the pony," he said to the two men. "But we'll be back."

"Where do you want to look now?" he asked Susan. "We've been all over the whole park."

"She's got to be here," said Susan. "The gate's closed, and that fence must be eight feet high." She waved her hand at the tall chain-link fence that ran all around the park. Beyond the tunnel building, she knew, were dense woods and private pasture land outside the town limits. Turning slowly in a full circle, Susan scanned the park. Somewhere within the fence, the pony had to be. She just had to.

"Maybe you just made her up," Kent said. "Maybe it was a phantom pony."

Susan snorted. She pointed to her jeans. Red horse hairs covered the insides of the legs. "Do they look like they came from a phantom?" she asked. "We've got to think about this. She's not out on the midway, so she must be back here somewhere. Or maybe there's a hole in the fence behind the trees. Let's go check."

They ran through the grove and followed the fence until it ended at the Tunnel of Terror building. There were no breaks in it, no place where a pony could have gotten through.

"She didn't get out through the fence," Kent said impatiently. "Let's forget about her and go get that free ride on the—"

"Wait! Look!" Susan grabbed his arm and pointed. Beyond the fence, in the dense underbrush of the wooded pasture, something moved. A flash of red showed through the green. A pony stepped out, grazing.

"There she is!" Susan cried. "No. Wait!" She looked again. This pony was beautiful, too, and had the same bright bay coloring. But it was bigger than the pony Susan had ridden and had a broad white blaze on its face.

Susan said with excitement, "That's a different pony, but it's the same kind as mine."

"*Yours,*" Kent teased. "How did she get to be *yours* all of a sudden?"

"Well, you know what I mean." Susan had no time for Kent's kidding. Not now. "These aren't ordinary ponies, Kent. I think they're show ponies. There must be a stable over there, somewhere. Let's go look."

3

The Search for Foxfire

Kent and Susan stared at the fence top high above their heads.

Kent said, "We'll have to climb it or else go around by the road."

Susan knew that would take a long time. And then it would take even longer to find the ponies.

They would have to climb the fence.

She took a deep breath. "I can if you can," she said, and began climbing.

"I can if you can," replied Kent. He quickly checked his shoelaces and then started after her.

Together they began climbing the fence, digging their fingers and toes into the small holes in the wire. At the top, sharp points of wire fence stuck up, ready to scratch them. Susan drew in her breath. It was going to be tricky to get over the top without losing her balance and falling. But Kent was watching. She had to do it.

The ground was a long way down. Slowly, Susan reached over the top with one arm. One leg went over, then the other. Finally she was on her way down on the other side. Kent was close behind her. As they dropped to the ground, the blaze-faced pony jumped and galloped away.

"Come on," Susan said. "Let's follow him."

Through the long grass they ran, around clumps of bushes and under huge shade trees. Soon they were heading downhill into a narrow, hidden valley. There Susan stopped suddenly and whispered, "Look!"

A mare, almost like Susan's but a darker red, stood watching them. At her side was a newborn colt. He had a woolly red coat, huge dark eyes, and very long legs. It was the first colt Susan had ever seen, and she was fascinated. She held out her hand, and the colt stretched his nose toward her. He took a timid step in her direction.

"Come on," Kent said. Susan left the colt, but she sighed as she walked away.

"Someday, when I grow up, I'm going to have ponies like these. And a colt like that one," she said.

"And I'm going to have my own helicopter!" Kent got a faraway look in his eyes, a look Susan knew well. He loved helicopters as much as she loved ponies, and he had as many helicopter models as Susan had model horses.

They climbed out of the little valley and found themselves in an open pasture. Susan saw more ponies grazing—three here, two over there. A little group stood quietly up ahead. In the distance she and Kent could see a group of buildings surrounded by white wooden fences.

Without a word, they moved toward the buildings. As they got closer, Susan could tell that the biggest one was a stable. Beside it was a training ring, like a tiny race track. A pony was pulling a cart around it. Susan and Kent ducked so that the man driving the cart wouldn't see them.

"He might not like us being in his pasture," Susan whispered.

Kent whispered back, "Maybe we'd better get out of here."

"No, wait. Let's peek in the stable first. I want to see what it looks like inside. This has to be where my pony came from, don't you think?"

"I don't know," Kent whispered back. "I didn't see your pony. But if she's the same color—"

"It's a lot more than color. It's the way she looks, and prances, and just . . . everything. Come on! Let's look inside while that man is still out on the track."

They crept along till they got to the back of the stable. Peering in the windows, they saw box stalls—some empty, some with graceful red ponies in them. Through the last window they saw not a stall, but a tack room.

It was beautiful. The walls were pine-paneled. There were leather chairs and horse-print curtains. All along one wall hung black bridles and harnesses, their silver buckles gleaming. Another wall was covered with blue ribbons from horse shows and shelves of trophies. There were photographs, too, of show ponies hitched to fancy carts, being awarded trophies and huge rosettes.

One picture caught Susan's eye.

"That's my pony!" she said. "I'm almost positive."

Lettering under the photo said, "Foxfire of Summer Valley, Fine Harness Pony Champion, Indiana State Fair."

"Foxfire," Susan whispered, more to herself than to Kent.

Suddenly she wanted to get back to the park. She knew, now, where the pony came from. The important thing was to find Foxfire and get her safely back to her owner.

"Let's go," she said. They moved quickly, running when they could, across the open pasture, down into the tiny hidden valley. They slowed to a walk through the dense woods near the back of the tunnel building. Here the underbrush was so thick they could only see a few yards in any direction.

"Wait a minute," Kent puffed. "Got to tie my shoe."

Susan fumed with impatience. It seemed she'd spent half of her life waiting for Kent to tie his silly floppy double knots.

When he stood up, he said, "You know, we should have told that man at the stable that one of his ponies was in the park."

Susan's heart sank. Of course Kent was right. That's exactly what they should have done. Why hadn't she thought of it herself?

She hated it when he was right and she was wrong.

They could go back now and tell him, she thought. But then Foxfire's owner would probably come to the park and find the pony himself.

More than anything, Susan wanted to be the one. She imagined finding the pony and leading her back to the man at the stable. He would be grateful. So grateful that he would tell Susan she could come and ride Foxfire—anytime.

4

Trapped

"Look. The tunnel." Susan grabbed Kent's arm and pointed. The underbrush was so dense here, they were almost on top of the building before they saw it. Susan looked left and right, but couldn't see through the bushes in either direction. There was no way they could guess which end of the tunnel building they were nearest to.

Shrugging and looking at each other, they finally started moving to the left, working their way through the brambles with the tunnel wall close on their right.

"Ratty looking, isn't it?" Kent said, and Susan had to agree. The back of the building looked nothing like its brightly painted front. Back here, where no one ever saw, the boards were unpainted, and some were badly rotted.

Kent stopped so suddenly Susan banged into his back. Just ahead was a huge dead tree. Barkless, silvery gray, and almost as tall as they were, it was lying on its side with chunks of earth still hanging from its roots. But the top of the tree was out of sight—inside the Tunnel of Terror building.

"It must have blown over in the storm last night," Kent said.

When it fell, the tree had knocked down a section of the tunnel building's back wall. Susan and Kent ran toward the tree and the hole it had made.

"There. Look." Susan pointed to the ground beside the tree. A set of dainty pony tracks led into the dark hole of the tunnel building and disappeared.

"That's how she got into the park," Kent said. "But where is she now?"

"Probably trying to get out the same way she got in," Susan said. She was trying to think what the pony would be doing in the dark.

"She must have wandered in here. Then she got lost. Maybe she followed the train tracks till she came out the front. From there, she would have seen the other ponies. So she would have gone over to be with them."

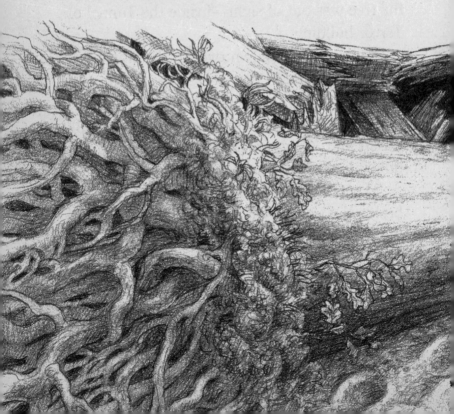

"Wouldn't someone have seen her?" Kent asked.

Susan thought about it. "She might have come in during the night, after the storm. If the tree blew down then, she would have had lots of time to wander into the tunnel building, come out on the midway, and find the other ponies. Anyone seeing her this morning would have thought she was one of Jackson's ponies. Like I did."

"And Jackson probably didn't even have his eyes open long enough to see anything," Kent added, laughing.

"Right. And when she ran away from me, she probably came back into the tunnel."

Kent went on, "And the tunnel man didn't see her, because he was so busy with the mechanic in the control room. So, now that we've figured everything out, let's go back and get our free ride on the tunnel train."

Susan put out her hand and caught his arm. She pointed to the muddy ground beside the tree. There was only one set of hoof prints.

"She went in through here, but she hasn't come out. And we couldn't find her in the park. That means she must be in the building somewhere." The thought made Susan freeze in sudden fear: her pony wandering loose in that huge dark building, and the ride man saying, "We'll be starting up the train pretty soon."

A high-strung show pony would panic at the sudden racket of the train, and at the scary things that popped up, shrieking and moaning, to terrify the passengers. Foxfire could hurt herself running around in there in fright. She might even get killed. "Kent, we've got to find her. Right away! The train!"

"Shouldn't we go tell the ride guy?" Kent asked.

They probably should, Susan thought. But she wanted, so badly, to find the pony herself.

"Come on," she said. "It'll only take a minute to find her and get her out of the building. Then we'll tell the ride man about the tree."

Kent didn't say anything. Instead, he followed her as she plunged through the hole into the tunnel, over broken boards and shattered dead branches. He stopped when she did, so their eyes could adjust to the dark.

Susan could see the metal tracks, and at either side of them, big wooden shapes rising almost to the roof. She knew what they were. They were the backs of the painted scenes.

Susan had been a passenger on the ride many times. She knew that as the train came close to each scene, lights went on suddenly and figures loomed and leaped over the riders in the train. There were skeletons, a head without a body, a body without a head, owls that hooted and flew. These scary scenes were placed where the tracks turned suddenly, so the riders got the feeling that they were going to run right into them.

The rest of the building, away from the tracks and scenes, was just big, dark, and empty.

Susan and Kent moved toward the tracks. They could see a sparkle in the dim light. It was water. The tracks disappeared in a shallow pool. When the train came along here the riders would be splashed.

Susan whispered, "I'll bet the pony smelled the water and came here to get a drink."

"Why are you whispering?" Kent asked. But he whispered too.

Susan opened her mouth to answer. Then a sound caught her attention. She listened. There it was again. A pony was whinnying.

"She must be scared!" Susan said. "Come on."

They went as fast as they could, but they were far away from the tree-hole now, and there was no light anywhere. Susan fell over an electric cable on the ground. Kent ran into a corner of a scary scene.

"I don't know about you," he said. "But I'm lost."

"Shh," Susan hissed. Silence. Then a small sound—breathing. Fast, shallow breathing, just ahead and to the right.

"Foxfire?" Susan called softly.

A sound came back, half snort, half nicker. Relief washed over Susan like a waterfall.

"She's here," Susan breathed. "Wait, let me try to get up to her. She'll be scared out of her mind. We don't want her to bolt again."

Cautiously she moved forward, her hand

outstretched. Her fingertips brushed warm silk. The pony stood.

"I've got her," Susan whispered, wrapping her arms around the pony's neck. Then she felt...something wrong. The neck muscles were bunched hard. The pony didn't move...or couldn't.

With no light to see by, Susan could only feel. She ran her hand over Foxfire's shoulder and down her leg. The leg jerked under her touch, but didn't move. Couldn't move. Farther down the leg, Susan's fingers found the answer.

The small hoof was caught between two crosspieces of the narrow track. Susan pulled on the hoof and tried to move the crosspieces, but she couldn't get the pony's foot loose. "Kent," she gasped, "she's stuck!"

Then they both heard it—a clattering roar that seemed to shake the whole building. The tracks began to vibrate.

"Oh, no," Kent cried. "They've started the train!"

5

Tunnel of Terror

After her first jolt of panic, Susan's mind started to work. She had to get out to the front of the building to stop the train. Otherwise, in just a few minutes, it would round the bend and hit Foxfire.

She wanted to stay with the pony, but she knew she could run faster than Kent. He was younger and smaller than Susan, and not quite as brave—though he'd never admit it.

Quickly she said, "You stay here and keep trying to get her foot loose. I'll go stop the train." Before Kent could answer she was on her way.

Then lights glared and hollow laughter boomed. A witch, arms outspread, loomed toward Susan. Her gray green face was covered with warts, her mouth stretched in an evil grin.

Susan's heart jumped. She stumbled backward. The light and sound switched off, and the witch became a dummy again, slumped in its dark box.

More slowly, more carefully, Susan moved ahead, feeling her way along the tracks with her feet. She tried as hard as she could to remember how the ride went. Was the water-splash near the beginning or near the end? She couldn't remember. She knew the track looped back and forth inside the building. It turned and twisted like a maze. But where was the entrance?

She could hear the train somewhere off to her left. The sound made her break into a faster walk. Then she started to run again. "I've got to get out there and stop the train," she thought.

She tripped and fell forward against wire

mesh. Suddenly green lights flashed on and a bloody head flew toward her, screaming and grinning. Susan could hardly keep from screaming herself. She knew it was only part of the ride, but her mouth was dry anyway and her pulse raced. She went on.

In the distance the train rumbled. "It's coming closer," thought Susan. Then a giant bat
flew at her face, fangs dripping blood.

Suddenly the train was clattering toward
her. She jumped aside as it passed. In the flash-
ing light from a scary scene, Susan saw the ride

man and the mechanic in the train's front seat.

"Stop the train!" she yelled as loud as she could. But her voice was lost in the shriek of a skeleton.

She started to run. Seconds counted now. The train was getting closer to the place where Foxfire was caught.

Susan rounded another turn. There, just ahead of her was a crack of light. The doors! The swinging doors that led outside to the platform...and the big red lever!

Susan ran to the lever and pulled. Nothing happened. Panic threatened to overwhelm her. She pushed it the other way. Gears creaked, and the lever moved. Somewhere inside the building, the clattering of the train slowed down. She moved the lever again, all the way back. There was a screech of metal on metal, and the noise from the train stopped. Relief washed over her. The train was stopped. But...had it stopped in time?

It seemed to take forever to find her way

back. Then, far ahead, she saw a glow of light, and heard voices. She listened, but there was no scream of pain from Foxfire...Susan stumbled, caught herself, and ran on.

The train had stopped just three feet from the terrified pony. Susan could see the white-rimmed eye, the gleam of panic-sweat on

Foxfire's hide. The beam of the mechanic's flashlight played on the two men, who were staring down at the pony's hoof. Then the mechanic disappeared into a dark corner of the building and, a few seconds later, the lights came on. For the first time, Susan really saw the inside of the tunnel building. With the lights on, the building looked shabby and ordinary. The skeletons and floating heads were all strung with wires, like puppets. And it was smaller than she had imagined.

But that wasn't important now. Susan moved close to Foxfire. Stroking the silky mane, she tried to calm her pony.

The mechanic had gotten his toolbox and was already taking off the bolts that held the crosspieces.

The ride man looked at Susan. "I couldn't figure out why the train stopped, but it's a good thing it did. Another few feet and we'd have hit that pony."

"Didn't you see me?" Susan asked him.

"Didn't you hear me when I yelled to you to stop the train?"

"We saw you," the ride man said.

Kent laughed. "They thought you were one of the spooks, Susan." She hit at him, and then started laughing herself. She felt weak and silly with relief, now that the tension was broken.

The ride man went on. "We couldn't hear what you said, and we couldn't stop the train. That lever out front is the only thing that will do it. And of course we had no way of knowing this animal had gotten into the building and was on the tracks."

"Here we go," said the mechanic. He loosened the crosspiece, and Foxfire pulled her hoof free.

Susan let out her breath and leaned against the pony. She could feel fear, like electricity, tingling beneath the silky skin. "Easy, girl. It's all over now." The pony rested her head against Susan's chest and gradually relaxed.

No matter what anyone said, this was

Susan's pony. She and Foxfire knew it.

Kent looked at the train, puzzled. Finally he said, "If you can only work the train from that lever outside, how did you get it started? And how would you have stopped it when you were through?"

The ride man grinned. "The train starts off slowly. I can throw the lever, start running, and jump in before the train picks up speed. As it comes out of the building, the train has an automatic slowdown. I can jump out, throw the lever, and bring it to a safe stop. Of course, when the park is open, there's always someone out there to work the lever."

The ride man said to Susan, "You kids better take that pony back out through the hole. When we came around in the train, we saw what happened to the wall. There's a pony farm back there. That's probably where she came from."

"I don't have anything to lead her with," said Susan. She still had her arms around

Foxfire's neck, but she couldn't safely lead the pony that way, not without the risk of having her take fright and break away again.

"Here," Kent said. Swiftly he sat and began ripping the overlong laces from his shoes and tying them together. They were just long enough to loop around Foxfire's neck and give Susan a handhold.

Susan couldn't help laughing. This made up for all the times she'd waited impatiently for

Kent to tie the stupid things. She led the pony toward the back of the building, and Kent followed, trying to keep his shoes on by curling his toes.

The mechanic said, "Wait. We'll come with you. We'll have to put something across that hole, to keep the ponies out until we can get the wall fixed."

As Susan led Foxfire through the broken wall into the woods, she saw a man coming toward them through the underbrush. It was the same man who had been driving the cart at the stable.

"Foxy!" he called in a happy voice.

"She got into the park," Susan told him. "We were just bringing her back to you. She's not hurt or anything."

Susan fell silent and leaned against Foxfire's shoulder. It was all over now. Foxfire wasn't her pony anymore. It was time to give her back to her real owner. The ache in Susan's throat was a little bit of pride, a lot of sadness.

The ride man said, "You've got these kids to thank that the pony isn't hurt, or worse. They were the ones who found her. The pony had caught her hoof on the track and couldn't get loose. We were running the train around, to check it before the park opens tomorrow. If this little girl here hadn't run all the way through the Tunnel of Terror and pulled the lever to stop the train, your pony would have been hit for sure."

"Caught on the track?" The man's jaw dropped. "I just now saw that downed tree, the hole in the wall there. I was afraid Foxy might have wandered through it. She's the most curious pony I've ever had. The smart ones always are—they're just like kids."

He paused, and swallowed, and looked suddenly shaken. "Had her hoof caught in the track, did you say? She could have...oh..." Susan could almost see the horrible images passing through the man's mind. It was obvious that he cared very much about his ponies.

He went to Foxfire and ran his hands over her, checking the bruised foot, calming her with his touch. He looked up then, and his eyes met Susan's, across Foxfire's back. "Thank you," he said, his voice heavy with emotion.

He replaced the shoelace loop with the lead rope he carried and drew Foxfire to him. "If anything had happened to her...makes me sick to think about it," he said. "I'll get all these

ponies into the other pasture till that wall is fixed."

To Susan, he said, "Foxfire and I owe you a lot. What's your name? I'm Jim Reed, Summer Valley Hackney Stable."

"Susan Greenway, Six-twelve Sycamore Lane. And this is Kent Hull. He helped a lot."

Kent took a step toward the handshake, stumbled on the flopping tongue of his shoe,

and caught himself just in time. "Pleased to meet you," he said, as they all laughed.

Mr. Reed shook Kent's hand, then Susan's. It was Susan's first adult handshake. The man was smiling down at her so warmly she didn't want to let go.

"I rode her," Susan blurted out. "I thought she was one of Jackson's ponies so I rode her. But then I knew she was different. Better. She just floated me through the air."

The words sounded silly, but Mr. Reed nodded. "Our ponies aren't used to being ridden," he said. "We show them as fine-harness ponies. But you're right. They are quality animals and they know it. I just wish I was light enough to ride them myself." He patted Foxfire's neck fondly.

"Well, thank you again, Susan," he said. "It was a pleasure meeting you." He offered his hand for another shake.

"And if you'd like to come over sometime and ride Foxfire, I'm sure she'd enjoy it."

As if to say she would, Foxfire leaned over and tickled Susan's neck with her soft whiskers.

Susan grinned so hard she couldn't speak. She could only nod, hard and fast, her eyes bright with joy. Mr. Reed understood.

The pony seemed to understand, too. She rested her chin on Susan's shoulder and gave a contented sigh.

"I'll see you soon, Foxfire," said Susan.

About the Author

"I dreamed of having a horse of my own the whole time I was growing up," says LYNN HALL. "I finally got one when I was fourteen—after years of wishing and whining and saving my money." Lynn Hall is the author of more than eighty-five books for children and young adults, including the Stepping Stone Book *The Mystery of Pony Hollow*. She lives in Iowa, where she breeds and shows champion Bedlington terriers and continues to write.

About the Illustrator

MARIE DEJOHN comes from a family of artists and has always loved to draw. "While I was growing up," she says, "I couldn't wait to wake up and start drawing. I drew a picture every day before breakfast." Since then, Marie DeJohn has illustrated many books for children. She lives in Connecticut with her two cats, Buddy and Tahini, who like to lounge on her drawing table and watch her at work.